First published in Swedish as *Duktiga Annika*
First published in English in 2009 by Floris Books
15 Harrison Gardens, Edinburgh
www.florisbooks.co.uk
Third printing 2012
© Bonnier Carlsen Bokförlag 2008
English version © Floris Books 2009
British Library CIP Data available
ISBN 978-086315-649-6
Printed in Belgium

Emily and Daisy

Elsa Beskow

Floris Books

Once, there was a little girl called Emily, who lived with her mummy and daddy in a red cottage in the country.

Emily helped Mummy with lots of things. She shooed the flies away when Mummy was milking Daisy the cow. She could also dress herself, wash her face, brush her hair, set the table and sweep the floor.

One day, Mummy was baking and Emily was playing with her elephant, her doll and her little wagon. Mummy was worried.

"There's a hole in the fence, Emily, and I'm afraid that Daisy the cow will run through it," said Mummy.

"Are we going to mend the hole?" asked Emily.

"Yes, Daddy will mend it tonight, but if Daisy gets into the clover field, she might eat too much clover and become very ill."

"Don't worry Mummy," said Emily. "I'll go to the meadow and look after Daisy."

She got her little bucket to take with her but couldn't find her spade.

Emily set off down the path to the meadow. After a while, she met a big dog.

"Woof woof. Are you scared of me?" asked the dog.

"Not at all," replied Emily. "You look like a friendly dog. I'm going to the meadow to look after Daisy the cow."

"Come with me instead," said the dog, "and we can watch some rabbits."

"No, thank you," said Emily.

"Well, goodbye then," said the dog. "Let me know if you need help with Daisy."

Emily thanked him and continued along the path.

Next, she met Billy the Boaster.

"Where are you going?" asked Billy.

"To the meadow to look after Daisy the cow," replied Emily.

"Come with me instead," said Billy, "and we can do some fishing. I'll catch a fish twice as big as Daisy!"

"No, thank you," said Emily and continued along the path.

Soon, Emily reached the gate to the meadow, but the bolt was too high and she couldn't open it. An old man with a sack on his back came along.

"What are you doing?" asked the man. "Leave that gate alone."

"I need to get into the meadow to look after Daisy the cow," replied Emily.

"I see," said the man. "Sorry if I scared you. Let me open the gate." And he did. He also gave her a nice new wooden spoon out of his sack. "You can use it with your bucket," he said.

Emily said thank you.

In the meadow, Emily said hello to Daisy the cow and noticed the hole in the fence. It was near to a sandpit Daddy used to get sand for the paths. Emily sat down and started making sandcastles with her bucket and new wooden spoon.

Daisy wandered up, sniffed at a sandcastle and knocked it over.

"Naughty Daisy!" cried Emily and hit Daisy on the nose with her spoon. Daisy jumped back, turned and ran through the hole in the fence, into the clover field.

Emily ran after her. "Come back!" she shouted, but Daisy didn't listen and ran further into the field. The clover was very tasty and she wanted to eat more and more.

Emily caught Daisy's tail and pulled it, but Daisy was stronger and pulled Emily along. Emily ran behind, crying. "Help!" she shouted.

All of a sudden, the friendly dog appeared. "Woof woof woof," he barked, running towards Daisy and guiding her back through the hole in the fence, into the meadow.

"Oh, thank you, thank you!" cried Emily.

"You're welcome. It was nothing," said the dog, and he ran home.

Emily wanted to mend the fence straight away so that Daisy wouldn't run off again. She noticed some fence poles sticking out of a heap of twigs and started to pull them out.

"What are you doing?" shouted a little voice. Emily saw a little old elf pulling on the other end of the pole. "If you pull out these poles, my roof will fall down," he said.

"I need to mend the fence," said Emily.

"I see," said the elf. "Sorry if I scared you. Let me find some more poles and I'll mend the fence for you. Come on children!"

Then Emily saw a small doorway in the pile of twigs with five elf children staring out at her.

The elves brought some long poles and the little old elf started to mend the fence. The elf children stared at Emily's sandcastles and laughed as they climbed on the heaps of sand. Emily laughed too and made more sandcastles around them.

An elf woman tugged on Emily's dress. "Can I borrow your bucket," she asked, "to get a little milk from Daisy the cow? We want to make pancakes."

"Pancakes, pancakes!" cried the elf children, jumping up and down.

"Alright," said Emily, "but just a little bit of milk."

The elf woman thanked her and took the bucket. In a flash, she was back with the milk, then disappeared into the twig house.

"The fence is completely mended," said the old elf. "I hope you'll leave my roof alone now. Would you like to share our pancakes with us?"

"Pancakes, come and eat pancakes!" cried the elf children.

"They smell delicious," said Emily, "but the door is too small. I won't fit through it."

"Come and try!" said the elf children, pulling and pushing Emily towards the house.

Just then, Emily heard her mother's voice calling. "Emily, where are you?"

"I'm here, Mummy." As soon as Emily said the words, the elf children disappeared into the twig house and the door closed. At Emily's feet was her bucket, full of wild strawberries.

Mummy came through the gate to milk Daisy the cow. "Look, Mummy," said Emily, "here's a new wooden spoon, the fence is mended and I have a bucket full of wild strawberries!"

Mummy was very pleased. They milked Daisy while Emily told her the whole story.

On the way home, they met Billy the Boaster. He had only caught one little fish.

"Did you pick those strawberries?" he asked.

"No, I got them from the wood elves," replied Emily.

"If they picked strawberries for me, I'd want a big bucketful, not a little bucket like that," said Billy.

"Well, you didn't catch a fish the size of Daisy, did you?" laughed Emily. Billy didn't know what to say.

That evening, everyone had wild strawberries for supper, with cream and sugar. Daddy said they were the best strawberries he'd ever tasted.

After supper, Emily got a bone and some sugar lumps, and took them to the friendly dog who had helped with Daisy the cow. The dog was happy to see her, and together they watched the rabbits playing as Emily gave them the carrots she had brought for them.

Then Billy came along.

"I suppose your rabbits are as big as elephants?" laughed Emily.

"No," said Billy. He had stopped boasting because it was a silly thing to do. They had fun feeding the rabbits together.

Every so often, they heard a long "mooo" from the meadow. It was Daisy the cow, asking where all the tasty clover had gone.